Juvie

a novel

by

PAUL KROPP

H·I·P Books

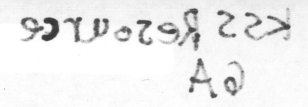

Library and Archives Canada Cataloguing in Publication

Kropp, Paul, 1948–
  Juvie / Paul Kropp.

(New Series Canada)
ISBN 1-897039-16-6

  I. Title. II. Series.

PS8571.R772J89 2006   jC813'.54   C2006-900842-6

General editor: Paul Kropp
Text design: Laura Brady
Illustrations drawn by: Catherine Doherty
Cover design: Robert Corrigan

  2 3 4 5 6 7

Printed and bound in Canada by Webcom

High Interest Publishing acknowledges the financial support of the Government of Canada through the Book Publishing Industry Development Program (BPIDP) for our publishing activities.

What's it really like inside a juvenile detention centre? Russ was innocent. He just wants to keep his nose clean. But the other guys don't make that easy.

CHAPTER 1

Got to Sound Tough

"I didn't do it."

Those were my first words in Juvie. *I didn't do it*. I didn't steal that car, not like the cops said. I didn't drive it as crazy as they said. I'm not that stupid.

But nobody believed me. Nobody backed me up. So then I was in Juvie, doing the first part of a two-year sentence. I'd be stuck here for a couple of months, a year at most, and then they'd send me to a group home. "That should teach you a lesson," the judge said. But what was the lesson? I was just a guy in the wrong place at the wrong time with the wrong friends.

"I shouldn't be here." Those were my second words in Juvie. I was talking to my roommate, a guy called Mouse.

"I heard that line before," Mouse said.

"You calling me a liar?" I shot back. *Got to sound tough*, I told myself. You can't let the other guys think you're weak. You've got to pretend that you're tough, even if you're scared to death.

Mouse smiled at me. He had bad teeth, so his smile didn't look too good. In fact, Mouse didn't look too good at all. He had greasy hair and tiny eyes behind thick glasses. His chin kind of faded away into his neck. Only his ears were big, so maybe that's why he was called Mouse.

"I'm not calling you nothing," Mouse replied. "I'm just saying, I heard that before. Here in Juvie, half the guys didn't do it. The other half of the guys are proud of what they did."

"Which half are you in?"

"I'm in the middle. I did what I did, but I don't brag about it." Mouse laid back on his bed and looked up at the ceiling. The ceiling had a vent, a light and a sprinkler to put out fires. It was pretty dull, but so were the walls.

"So what did you do?" I asked him.

"Trashed a house," he said like it was nothing at all. "Got a little carried away with a baseball bat. You know how it goes."

"Whose house?"

There was a little pause before Mouse answered. "My dad's."

I didn't say a thing, but there must have been a question in my eyes.

"The old man was off with one of his girlfriends, so I got a little bored. Maybe I was trying to make a point or something. That's what the shrinks tell me. Not a lot of eight-year-olds smash all the windows in their own house."

I tried to picture Mouse as an eight-year-old. He was small and skinny for a kid of sixteen, but he must have been tiny at eight. He must have really wigged out to go wild like that.

Of course, I was no angel when I was that age. There was no halo over my head back then, no gold stars on my report card. I stole my first car when I was nine, or maybe ten, and drove it a couple of blocks. I was a pretty good driver for a little kid, but it took a long time to become a good car thief. By the time I was eleven, I had it down. I couldn't boost those BMWs and Jags with all the alarms. They were too tough. But I could steal most cars, no sweat. I even had a deal with this old guy who'd pay me to steal. He'd tell me what he wanted – a certain kind of SUV, or maybe a certain color Honda. That stuff was easy.

I got caught a couple of times. The cops don't do much to you the first time. You get a lecture and a ride home, and then your mom gives it to you good. But the second time you get caught, the courts take over. You get the group home or the foster home. That's when I got smart. It's not like my house is all that great, but it beats a foster home. The only place I ever got beat up was in a foster home.

So I gave up stealing cars at age twelve. Honest.

I told that to the cops and the judge this last time, but they didn't believe me. It's like a kid gets marked for life. *This kid is trouble*, is what people said about me. But I wasn't that much trouble. I had made up my mind to get straight, and I did – really, I did.

"So you've been here for eight years?" I asked Mouse. I knew that couldn't be true. Most guys are here for less than a year.

"In and out," Mouse replied with a yawn. "Sometimes they tell me I'm ready for the big world out there and they send me home, but I don't last long. I kind of like it here, you know? You get decent food and a TV that works and the staff even likes me. It's better than being at home."

"You've got to be nuts," I told him.

He got off his bed and smiled at me. "Yeah, that's what they say." He got this kind of crazy look on his face. "But what's wrong with being nuts?"

This guy is weird, I said to myself. I went over to my bed and grabbed a book from the shelf. It was a great book called *Holes*. I loved that book even before the movie came out, so I began reading it

again. No matter how bad things might get at Juvie, they were better than the camp in *Holes*.

"Hey, I saw that movie," Mouse said to me. "You a good reader?"

"Yeah, pretty good," I told him. That was true. I wasn't a great student, but I was good at reading and math.

"I don't read so good," Mouse admitted. "The teachers here, they keep trying to get me to read better but it never seems to work. I think I've got dys-whatever . . . what's that word?"

I didn't say anything. I didn't know the word either.

"Anyhow, I got a deal for you," Mouse said. "I'll kind of show you the ropes around here, since I know them better than anybody. I'll tell you how to stay out of trouble and what guys to watch out for. I'll tell you which staff guys you can trust and which guys will stab you in the back."

"So what do I do for you?" I asked.

"Read me that book out loud," he said. "I mean, you're gonna read it for yourself, so it's no big deal to read a little to me."

I thought about this for a second. I wasn't sure that I liked Mouse and I wasn't sure I could trust him much. But I'd never been in Juvie before, and from what I'd heard it was pretty awful. I could use somebody who knew how the place worked. I mean, if somebody as small as Mouse could survive here, then I could get by.

"Okay. Deal," I told him.

"So here's your first bit of advice," he replied. "Watch out for Stick Man – that's our nickname for this staff guy named Steve. Stick Man is mean as anything. Give him any excuse, and you'll pay big time. You got to be careful and you got to be smart."

"Thanks," I told him.

"Okay, now it's your turn."

I opened the book and began. *"There is no lake at Camp Green Lake . . . ."*

CHAPTER 2

The Guys of C Wing

"Get your butts out of bed!" came the shout. "Move it!"

It was my second day in Juvie. Just to be clear, the real name of this place isn't Juvie. This is the Broken Arrow Correction Centre for Young Offenders. That's me, a young offender. All of us in here must have offended somebody, like big time. We were young, too. That meant we were too young to go to real jails or the pen. Until you're

18, they don't make you do hard time in the pen. The courts send you to a place like this. Juvie is supposed to straighten us out. It's supposed to make us decent guys.

That's a laugh, of course. It would take a miracle to make some of these guys decent.

There are eight wings in this Juvie, each with ten to twelve guys. We were in C wing, right at the north end. The other wings all had letters, A to H. Seven of the wings are for guys, H wing is for girls. There is another wing that doesn't have a letter. We call it "The Hole." The staff call it "Up Front." If you get kicked out of A to H wings, you get sent Up Front. Mouse told me that it was real bad there. He said you get locked in a room, by yourself, all day and all night. If they give you a pencil to do school work, they take away your reading book. If they give you a book, they take away your pencil. Pretty nice, eh?

Each of the wings has five or six bedrooms, a middle room with a TV and an "honours" room with some couches and a pool table. The middle room is supposed to be like a family room. That's where the staff is. That's where guys could talk to each other.

The "honours" room is for the guys who get enough points. You get points for doing your homework or reading a book. You lose points for talking back or goofing off. If you try to make a break, or hit a staff guy, you lose all your points and get sent to The Hole. A guy stays in The Hole until staff decide to let him back.

In the centre of all the wings is the Hub. You get to it through the yard or through the tunnels. The Hub has classrooms, a wood shop, a gym and a place to eat. There used to be a weight room, but now only staff can use it. They don't want any of us bulking up bigger than they are.

We spent our nights in the wings. We spent a lot of our days in The Hub. It was where we met some of the guys from the other wings. It was the only time we even *saw* a girl.

After wake up, you get to take a shower. It's one guy at a time. I went first and got cleaned up. Mouse went after me. He looked even funnier with no glasses. When he came back to the room, I saw his arm for the first time. His right arm was all scarred and the skin was a strange dark purple color. Mouse saw me staring at it.

"Pretty ugly, isn't it?" he said, putting on a long-sleeved shirt. "A gift from my father."

"Like, how?"

"Boiling water on the stove," he said. "My dad says I spilled it on myself, but I kind of wonder. I was too little to remember."

"I guess you've got some problems with your father," I said.

"That's what the shrinks say," Mouse replied. By then he was dressed and we were ready to go.

There were two staff on duty that morning. One had a pass-card that said "Steve" so I knew he was Stick Man. He was a tall, thin guy with a scar on his chin. The other was an old guy with a big Polish name. He looked like Santa Claus without the red and white suit. Mouse told me his nickname was Pops.

That morning was my first real look at the other guys in C Wing. Over the next week, Mouse told me more about all of them.

The meanest guy was Jackson. He was a big, white kid with tattoos on both arms. He looked like he worked out to build up his arm muscles. Those muscles and the look on his face were enough to scare me. Mouse told me that Jackson was in for murder, though I had my doubts. Guys who were in for murder didn't get Juvie.

The biggest guy was Kareem. He was as tall as a Lakers' player and looked like he could chew me up and spit me out for breakfast. The funny thing was, Kareem was a really nice guy. He was polite, well-spoken and pretty smart. He got along with almost all the guys, even Jackson. Of course, Kareem was big enough to handle himself. A fight between Kareem and Jackson would be a tough contest.

Sig was the only guy who didn't look like he belonged in Juvie. Sig – short for Sigmund – was tall, blond and good-looking. He looked like those guys you see in teen mags for girls, all buff and smiling. The staff liked Sig. He got to work jobs at Juvie and make real money, like three bucks a day. The staff let him push a broom down the halls and mow the lawn in the yard.

Sig's only problem was that he was crazy. He had started drinking at age ten and then went downhill. Some guys get mellow drunk; Sig got crazy drunk. The second time he beat somebody up, he ended up in Juvie. Now he was going crazy again. This time he was going crazy trying to escape.

There were a couple of other guys, too, called Cutter and Dopey. Mostly they kept to themselves. With Mouse and me, we had seven guys in C Wing. There was room for three more, but I guess the courts were working a bit slow. We called the empty bedroom our "guest room." We joked that our buddies could use it if they stayed over to visit.

Some joke. In Juvie, you don't get many visits.

In the morning, the staff would line us up. One staff would be at the front and walk backwards. The other staff would be at the back, walking forwards. This was a rule the staff had – never turn your backs on the "clients." We were the clients. Maybe that was how they pretended this wasn't a jail.

For the next year of my life, I'd be "a client." Unless I got cleared, unless I could get out.

"It could be worse," Mouse told me.

"Yeah, how?"

"Imagine a group home run by my father."

CHAPTER 3

Two Lessons

We had school five days a week, six hours a day. It was just like real school except the classes were small. The teachers were the usual bunch, some good, some bad. The only difference was the other students. In real school, the other kids might diss you or talk behind your back. In this school, the other kids would knife you if they had a chance.

They really could. There were at least a few

weapons at Juvie, not guns, but knives and Ninja stars. The guys made the Ninja stars in shop. Or some friend would sneak a knife in from outside. Mouse told me I could buy a blade from Jackson if I had twenty bucks. I just laughed. Where would I get twenty bucks? We got eight bucks a week as our "allowance," but then they took two bucks back for "savings." Nice. In a year, I'd have a hundred bucks. What a thrill.

We had classes in reading, math, science and shop – at least, those were my classes. Other kids had different classes. The teachers said it was all based on what a guy needed. They said we had to be winners in school to be winners in life.

We didn't even laugh. I looked at a guy like Dopey and tried to figure what he could do. Or even Mouse. Mouse wasn't dumb, but he couldn't read. I mean, what can you do in life if you can't even read?

They put me in the "red" group, which must mean *smart* because all of us were pretty sharp. There was me, two guys from G wing, Sig, Jackson and a girl. The girl was really something. I mean, most of the girls in H wing were pretty awful. They were stupid or skinny or mouthy or crazy. Some of them had been out on the streets, and it showed. A girl hits the streets at age 12 or 13 and she looks awful when she's 16. There were girls in H wing that looked 40, but they couldn't be older than 17.

But not this one girl. She had a name, Jenna, that I kind of liked. Jenna had a real chip on her shoulder, but she wasn't messed up. You could tell she was smart, and she was always reading something. I like that. I like smart girls and girls with attitude. Jenna was something. Even in baggy clothes, you could tell she was something.

Mouse told me that Jenna was in for assault. She beat up some other girl, like bad, for some reason. Mouse told me that she wasn't a girl to fool around with. I said I'd take my chances.

The first day in class, I had to talk to the teacher. Her name was Ms. Mikos, or something like that, but we called her Gracie. She was kind of cute, for an older woman, and really skinny. The only really good thing was that she smelled good. The rest of Juvie smells like dog dirt, but Gracie smelled like flowers.

"So why are you here?" she asked.

"No good reason. I didn't do it, if that's what you want to know."

"Uh huh," she said, taking some notes on a piece of paper. "Car theft again?"

"So why do you ask me if you already know?" I shot back.

"Just checking," she replied, cool as ice. "What about that old guy?"

"I didn't hit the old guy," I told her. Now I was getting really mad.

24

"Just asking," she told me. "It was in the papers, but you never get the whole truth."

"Yeah, right."

"So what do you want, Russ?" she asked. It was the first time anybody had used my name, Russ.

"I want out of here," I told her.

"But what do you want out of life? What goals do you have?"

"I want out of here." I thought that was pretty funny. Gracie didn't even smile.

"Anything else?"

"That'll do for now," I told her.

Gracie sighed and leaned back in her chair. "You know what's wrong with running away from stuff? You don't have any direction. You're running in a circle so you end up where you started. You need some direction, Russ. You need someplace to get to."

I didn't say anything. Teachers have lectured me all my life. If the words were going to sink in, they would have done it by now. I didn't even know this lady. But here she was, talking like she had life all figured out.

So that was lesson number one. After that, I had

to read *Of Mice and Men*, this old book they had. The other kids were ahead of me, into Chapter 3, so I had to catch up.

My next lesson came a couple of days later. We were reading out this chapter in class, taking parts. We were pretty good, if I do say so myself.

After class, I stopped to talk to Jenna for a bit. I told her that she was a good actor, and she kind of smiled at me.

"You're not bad yourself," she said. "But you shouldn't talk to me like this, just the two of us."

"Why not?" I asked her.

She just laughed. "You'll find out, Russ. You'll find out."

That didn't make much sense. I mean, I was just talking to somebody from my class, that was all. It was no big deal. I wasn't making moves or anything like that. I was just talking, like I might talk to Mouse or Sig or Kareem.

But in Juvie you've got to be careful who you talk to.

"You, Jerk," Jackson said to me later on. We had just gotten back to C Wing.

"The name is Russ," I said.

"Yeah, I had it right," Jackson said. "From now on, you're Jerk. Got it?"

He poked me in the shoulder, and it hurt. The guy had made one of his fingernails really sharp, into a point. I could feel the nail slice into my skin.

Don't cross Jackson, Mouse had told me. *If he lays into you, back away. He can beat you up and nobody will care.*

"Okay, so call me Jerk," I said. I looked around, but the only staff was Stick Man. He was looking the other way.

"Good, we got that straight," Jackson said. "Nobody's got to get hurt."

"Right," I agreed.

"So listen up," he told me. His face was up close to mine, so I could feel the spit. "Don't go talking to Jenna, you hear me. You want to talk to her, you got to ask me first. Got it?"

"Yeah, got it," I said.

He backed off and went to his room. I stood there for a minute, shaking, then looked at my

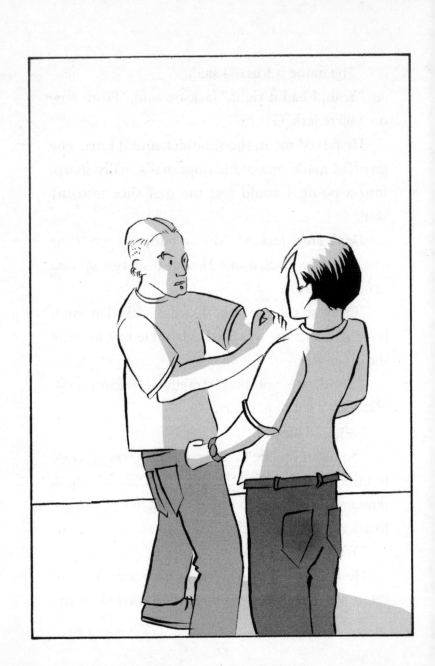

shirt. There was a rip in the cloth and a little blood where he'd poked me.

I looked over at Stick Man. He had seen the whole thing. He was the guy who should have stopped it right when it began. He was the guy who was supposed to stand up for guys like me. But Stick Man was just smiling. He was giving me a sick, sick smile.

That was lesson two . . . and lesson three.

CHAPTER 4

Something's Going Down

Sometimes you can forget that Juvie is a jail. If you're sitting in class, or eating in the meal room, it *feels* like a high school. You can pretend that your life isn't much different here. You can tell yourself that this is normal.

But Juvie isn't normal. The staff likes to pretend it's a school, or a summer camp, or a help centre. But the bottom line is security. The bottom line is that you can't get outside.

The teachers all have pagers and cell phones. The classrooms all have video cameras and hidden mikes. Each staff desk has a red pushbutton that calls for help. Each window is made of glass that won't break. Each door can be locked and unlocked from a desk at the front. Somebody is always watching.

After a while, you get used to it. The class walks up to a door and we wait. The door opens and we go forward a little. Then the first door closes and we wait. Then a second door opens and we go through. It takes a long time to walk down a hall like that.

Unless there's a lockdown. It was my third week in Juvie when we had our first lockdown. It was a great day outside, a warm October day. But inside, it all got weird. With no warning, all the doors got locked. Nobody could move – staff or kids. Suddenly all the staff's pagers and cell phones came out. Something was happening, but we didn't know what. Someplace, somebody was out of control. But we didn't know where and we didn't know who.

Later, I got the word from Mouse.

"Some guy in E wing made a run for it."

I looked at him, wondering. "And then?"

"Staff took him down, like hard," Mouse replied. "Now they've got him in body cuffs." Body cuffs are like handcuffs, but they tie up to a belt on your waist. They cut into your skin, like bad.

Trying to escape gets you sent to The Hole. It gets you put in cuffs. The only thing worse is hitting the staff. Only a fool takes a swing at staff, no matter how mad you get.

Of course, most of the staff are cool. For a lot of

us, they are the only guys on our side. They get to see us as we are, which isn't all that bad. A lot of the guys in here aren't bad, they're just hurting or messed up. There are a lot of guys like Mouse. There's nothing wrong with him that a decent family wouldn't fix. Too bad he doesn't have one. Not many of us do.

That night, I was reading Chapter 24 of *Holes*. It was my second time through the book. "*Stanley was half asleep when he got in line for breakfast. . . .*"

Mouse stopped me after the first sentence. "Hey, Russ, can I ask you something?"

"Yeah."

"How come you got sent here?" he asked. "I mean, car theft doesn't rate Juvie most of the time. You got to steal a lot of cars to be in here."

"Like I told you, I didn't do it. I gave up stealing cars, like four years ago."

"So what really happened?" he asked. "You don't look like a fighter or a crazy, so what was it?"

For a second, I wondered how much I should tell him. I'd kept my mouth shut for three weeks now. I'd kept my mouth shut before I went to court.

Never rat on your friends, I told myself. But my friends had gotten me into this.

"Bad timing, bad company," I said. I figured that was enough.

"Like what, like who?" Mouse asked. "I told you all about my lousy life, but you never say nothing."

"I'm a man of mystery," I said.

"Well, I don't like mysteries," Mouse said. "You tell me what really happened out there, and I'll tell you what's going down tomorrow."

I rolled over in bed and looked at him. "Like what?"

"You first," Mouse replied. "You talk to me and I'll tell you what I know."

I rolled back in bed and looked at the ceiling. Mouse was my only friend, the only guy I could talk to. I hadn't said much about my life. I hadn't told anyone what happened to me. Maybe it was time.

"Okay," I began. "I was hanging out with a bunch of guys. Years ago, I used to steal cars with some of them. We'd boost a car, go for a ride and then ditch the thing. We thought it was cool back then, but some of us grew up," I told him.

34

"Anyhow, there was this guy called Flick who was a real jerk. He was a new guy and kept saying that I'd lost my touch. Flick said all my stories about stealing cars were stupid. He was really dissing me, you know?

"So I said to myself, I'll show this jerk. I took all the guys out to a parking lot and said, you pick the car. They had to pick this Audi, so it was a tough boost. You need the codes to get into one of those. But I had my cell phone, so I made some calls. Pretty soon, the four of us were in that car and sailing down the road. I even let Flick drive. Maybe that was the stupidest thing. I let the jerk drive.

"Anyhow, it was a rainy night and you couldn't see much. We were heading down this one street and then I see this guy up ahead, riding a bike. It was dark, and he was in a dark coat, so I knew Flick didn't see him. 'Watch out for the guy,' I said, but Flick lost it. He slammed on the brakes, the car spun and hit the guy, and then we smashed into a parked car.

"The airbags went off, but I guess mine didn't work. When I opened my eyes, all the other guys

were gone. They'd run off. I wiped away a little blood, and then the cops were all over me. First time I ever had handcuffs on," I said.

"So did you tell them about Flick?"

I sighed. "I never rat," I told him. "I was the only guy in the car, so I took the fall. I didn't know the old guy would die, but then I got hit with manslaughter."

"Manslaughter – that can get you time in the pen," Mouse said.

I laughed. "Yeah, so I guess I'm lucky to be in Juvie."

For a second, Mouse didn't say much. I guess he was letting my story sink in. It was the first time I had told it to anyone. Maybe if I had told my lawyer, I wouldn't be here now. But there's no way you can replay your own life.

"Okay, my turn," Mouse said at last. "Tomorrow, at lunch, watch your back. Jackson and some guys in D wing are going to start something. Then there's going to be a break. If it happens, get down fast and stay down."

CHAPTER 5

Riot!

Staff won't let all of us eat meals at the same time. Half of us are still in class when the other half are in the meal room. They mix up the wings, too, so you never know who's going to be there.

Today it was C, D, G and H wings. That means the girls were there, at the far table. I sat with Mouse and Kareem, waiting. Sometimes I would look over at the H-wing table. That girl Jenna was sitting there, looking around, sometimes looking at me.

Was she trying to start something, or what?

Kareem whispered something to Mouse. I just waited.

"Ten minutes," Mouse quickly whispered to me. "Jackson gives the signal."

"Then what?"

"Don't know . . . just be ready."

So I pushed the food around on my plate. We had plastic spoons, forks and knives. Staff didn't trust us with anything that could be a weapon. But staff didn't know what the guys made in shop. They couldn't stop the stuff that came in from outside.

All I knew was this – if something started, I was getting down. I wasn't in on this, and I didn't need any more jail time. I never wanted to see The Hole. I didn't want to be put in cuffs or worse . . . the blanket. The blanket kind of smothers you, like a straight jacket. That would be the worst for me. I'd rather be shot.

I wondered how many guys knew what was coming. I wondered if Jenna was part of this, or just playing games. I looked at the four staff who were watching us. One of them was Stick Man. He

must have known about all this. But what about the other staff guys? What would they do? How much did they know?

Mouse reached into his pocket, then pulled out a piece of metal. I could feel him put it in my hand. It was a Ninja star.

"I don't want it," I told him.

"Just in case," he whispered.

"Don't be a fool," I whispered, handing it back.

Mouse shook his head and stuck the Ninja star under his leg. I couldn't figure out what he could do with it. If the staff guys came at us with their shields, the Ninja star would be useless. If Jackson or his guys came at us, it would just make them mad.

Still, Mouse was scared. He must have felt he had to do something, to get ready. Maybe if I knew what was coming, I'd feel the same way.

It was 12:22. I know that because I was watching the clock. Jackson got up and did this big yawn, stretching his arms out.

Then it all went crazy. For ten seconds, it all went crazy.

Jackson grabbed our table and flipped it over. That sent all the lunches and trays flying in the air, crashing down to the floor.

At the same second, the whole D wing ran at two of the staff. They had one staff guy down on the floor. The other staff was a woman who got pushed up against a wall.

A third staff guy was trying to call for help, but then Jackson got to him. He grabbed the staff guy around the neck and dragged him down.

That only left Stick Man, who looked at Jackson and then fell down. It was the most amazing thing. Nobody hit him. Nobody even got near him. But Stick Man was down on the floor like he'd been punched out.

"Move! Move! Move!" Jackson yelled out.

The guys in D wing began moving toward the east door as the siren went off. Jackson was right behind them. They had grabbed a pass-card from one of the staff guys, and that got them through the first door. Jackson dragged the last staff guy with them.

"Last chance, suckers," Jackson yelled to us.

Nobody moved. Jackson shook his head and joined the D-wing guys. They moved into the door passage, racing toward the way out.

But the siren was wailing. And then there was another sound: *click-smash-click-smash*. All the doors to our meal room were closing and locking. We were trapped inside.

Jackson and the D-wing guys were trapped, too. It was a lockdown. All of the doors in Juvie can be locked cold in a couple of seconds. Somebody had messed up. Not even a staff guy's pass-card will work in a lockdown.

The D-wing guys were screaming. The siren was wailing. The rest of us stood there, not sure what to do.

That's when a dozen staff guys showed up at the west door. I had never seen so many staff in one place at one time. They were looking at all of us, trying to figure out who was in this and who wasn't. Then there was a click, and the staff guys stormed into the meal room.

In Juvie, the staff don't have guns. But they're mostly big guys. They work out and get trained to

44

take down kids. And they have shields that can knock you to the floor.

"Down! Get down!" one staff shouted.

We fell to the floor, ducking under the table. I wasn't sure if Jackson had a gun. I didn't think the cheap plywood table would stop a bullet, but it might slow one down.

In a few seconds more, three of the staff guys were watching over us. The rest had gone over to the east door. Behind that door was Jackson, the staff guy Jackson held, and the D-wing guys.

"Let him go," shouted one of the staff guys. "Let him go or you're meat."

The D-wing guys were trapped. They couldn't get out.

There was a click and a sliding sound. The glass door between the staff guys and passage slid open. For a second, it was dead quiet. The staff guys held their shields up, ready to charge. The D-wing guys stared back at them.

Then one of the D-wing guys spoke. "Let him go, Jackson," he said. "It's over."

CHAPTER 6

Lockdown

"That was just stupid," I told Mouse.

"Not stupid," Mouse replied. "More like desperate."

We were locked into C wing, told to stay in our rooms. The honour lounge was closed. The TV was off. Meals came in on little plastic trays. There were no classes.

We were all being punished.

Mouse went on. "Some guys get kind of crazy in

here after a while. I mean, look at Sig. If he saw an open door, he'd be running so fast nobody could catch him. He's gone nuts. That must have happened to Jackson, too."

"Jackson has a girlfriend here," I said.

"So? He might have two or three outside. And outside, well, there's freedom," Mouse told me. "That don't mean much to me, but some of the guys would do anything to get it."

Freedom. It's not a word you think about much. You go to school, take a bus, see some friends, go to a party. None of that seems very special. But take that away – take freedom away – and you feel it. You feel it deep down. Outside, out in the real world, you can do what you want. Outside, you can do something different each day. You can go straight, go crazy, go quiet, go weird – but it's all up to you. Every day is a new day. Every day is full of things you can do.

In Juvie, every day is the same. You get up, shower, eat, march to school, eat lunch, march to your wing, march to dinner, march to your wing, watch TV, sleep.

Every day, the same.

If you wanted to change something, you couldn't. You didn't have a chance. You didn't have the power. Maybe that's the hardest lesson in Juvie – what it's like to be powerless. I mean, we couldn't even choose what we wanted to watch on TV. That was up to the staff. Just like the color of your pencil.

"Jackson didn't have a chance," I said.

"Maybe not, but he thought he did," Mouse said. "You saw that Stick Man was in on it. Maybe the staff guy in the control room was paid off. Maybe it was all set up and something went wrong at the last minute. Jackson wasn't stupid, but he might have been stabbed in the back."

"Stick Man?" I asked.

"Don't trust that guy. Not ever."

It took a week for Juvie to get back to normal. Jackson was gone, sent off to some other Juvie or maybe to the pen. Most of the D-wing guys were in The Hole. The rest of us never got the full story.

There was a payoff to somebody, by somebody. Somebody was going to check all this. Maybe they did. Maybe it takes a long time to lay the blame.

All we knew was that Stick Man was still around, still smiling.

In my LA class, we finished *Of Mice and Men*. Gracie, our teacher, said she wanted us "reds" to tackle a classic. That should have been my first clue that it would be bad. The second clue was when she said Shakespeare. And the third clue was *Romeo and Juliet*, of all the plays.

We did about two scenes a day. Sometimes we got to watch one of the movies, the old one or *Romeo Must Die*. Some days I got to be Romeo. Some days Sig got the starring role. Some days Kareem would do it. Jenna was always Juliet, and it kind of fit her. Except that Jenna would never kill herself for love, not like Juliet in the play.

"You miss him?" I asked her once.

"Who?" she replied, cool as anything.

"Jackson."

"He's just a guy," she said to me. "Now he's history." She said that with a shrug, with this cold

look in her eyes. It was like nothing made any difference.

"What about me?" I went on.

She gave me the same kind of cold look. "Just another guy," she sighed. "Don't let your role in the play go to your head."

Later that day, Sig found me back in C wing. He made sure that nobody could listen in.

"You like that girl, eh?" he began.

I didn't know what to say. Yeah, I liked Jenna, but I didn't really know her. In a place like Juvie, she was the nicest girl we had. So sure I liked her, but why should Sig care? It wasn't that I could do anything about it.

"Yeah, I guess," I said. I was being careful.

"She's not worth it," he told me. "I've heard a lot about Jenna, and it's mostly bad news. She's been on the streets and even knifed a guy. You gotta watch out with her."

From what I could figure, you had to watch out for almost everybody in Juvie. Jackson, Stick Man, Jenna – they were all bad news. Guys like Sig and Cutter were crazy. Guys like Mouse and Dopey were just sad cases. The only guys I could trust were Mouse and Kareem, and maybe our teacher Gracie – but you never could tell about staff.

"I'll be careful," I said.

There was a long pause. I don't think Sig really wanted to talk about Jenna. He had something else in mind.

"You ever think about getting out of here?" he asked.

"All the time," I told him. "Juvie makes my old high school seem like heaven."

"Yeah, but I mean like blowing this place. Breaking out."

This was Sig's big thing, at least that's what Mouse said. Sig was always talking about busting out. He kept coming up with plans to make a break. None of the plans worked out, but he never gave up. He was like this guy I knew who kept dreaming about getting a Porsche, but he only worked part-time at Sears. Dreams are cheap. In Sig's case, the dreams were close to crazy.

"Yeah, sure," I told him. I knew another crazy plan was coming up.

"I've got a new plan," he said. "You want in?"

The look on Sig's face was plain crazy. He had big blue eyes that just stared at you, like he was out of his mind. So you don't tell a crazy guy that he's crazy, because he might wig out. You just play along.

"Yeah, sure," I told him. "When you've got a way over the fence, just let me know."

Any guy who's locked up thinks about escape. It comes with the bars, the fences and the cameras. Escape! Got to find a way out of here! People who

are trapped are just like dogs in a cage: we want out. Juvie is like that, really. Despite the school and the social workers and all that, it's really just a big cage. The candy-cane fence out there isn't for Christmas. It's to make sure you can't get over the top and run.

But making a run for it is something else. There's security in Juvie, but not that much. The fence isn't a wall. It's not like the pen where they have guys with machine guns watching the wall. But if you run and get caught, you're toast. They double your sentence, or you get sent to a real jail.

And even if you could stay out, how could you live? For the rest of your life, you'd be looking over your shoulder. If you got pulled over for a speeding ticket, you'd be sweating bricks. Who wants to live a life like that?

So Jackson and Sig and guys like that – they're crazy. Like that old song, you can run but you can't hide. I had less than two years to go. No way I was going to make that four.

CHAPTER 7

Hostages

Nothing happened for a month. It was like Mouse said – Sig was crazy. He talked big, but never did much. "All talk, no action," was what Mouse said. That was true for the rest of us, too. In Juvie, there's a lot of talk but not much that a guy can do.

I got used to it. It's funny how something as strange as Juvie can come to feel normal. I only had a couple of visits and a couple of phone calls. That was my contact with the outside world. Visits and the TV – not much to keep a guy connected.

Mouse said I was lucky. Nobody ever came to see him. A lot of the guys here don't get visits. There's nobody outside who cares enough to come through the gates. Pretty sad, if you ask me. My family isn't great, but it's a real family. They come to visit a couple of times a month. My little sister even came to see me once. She asked me if I'd learned anything. I told her, "Be careful when you pick your friends." That was no joke. I wouldn't be here now if Flick were a real friend.

By November, I had Juvie all figured out. When a new guy would come in, I'd show *him* the ropes. I started to think about moving on to a group home next year. That could be good or bad, but it would be that much closer to the real world.

Then Sig whispered something to me before class.

"It's today," he whispered.

What's today? is the first thing I thought. We had a book review due for Gracie. In class, we were working on math more than LA. Maybe there was some test coming up that had slipped my mind.

"I'm out of here, today," he whispered again. "Got a guy waiting outside."

"Right," I said.

I guess Sig wasn't going to take me with him. He must have figured that I didn't want to make a break. I'd listen to him talk, but I wouldn't tell him to count me in. Besides, Sig was crazy. He'd been talking to Mouse about escape for more than a year. Nothing ever happened.

We got to class as usual. Jackson was gone, of course, but there were two new guys from D wing. Jenna was in her desk, putting on some lip gloss. She did that a lot, whether she needed lip gloss or not. Sig was in his seat, looking kind of tense. Some of the guys get like that here. Some part of their body – a leg or a hand – is always jiggling. It's like they have a muscle twitch. Anyhow, Sig was twitching, but he did that sometimes. The two new guys were working on some math. Gracie was with them, trying to give them some help.

I was doing some math problems in a workbook. I hate workbooks, but that's what we had. I was on page 36, question 3, when it all started.

"Hey!" shouted Gracie.

I looked up real fast and saw Sig moving fast. He grabbed Gracie's pager and then ran over to Jenna's desk.

"Nobody move," he said, looking at us and at the camera.

He pulled a knife from his sock and grabbed Jenna's arm.

"Nobody move or shout, or else she gets it," he said. He sounded nervous, almost high. No question – he was crazy enough to slice anybody who stood in his way.

My heart began racing. The idiot was actually going for it. Sig was trying to make a break.

Sig moved around behind Jenna, hiding the knife from the camera.

"You know they're watching," he told us, "so don't make any faces. Gracie, you just go along with this and nobody will get hurt. You got it?"

Gracie looked like all the blood had drained from her face. "Sig, you don't want to do this."

"You're right," he told her. "I don't *want* to do

this, but I've *got* to do this. I've got to get out of here." Then he turned to Jenna. "Okay, Jenna, you're coming with me. Don't make any big deal and it'll be fine." Sig brought the knife up, close to Jenna's neck.

Jenna turned as white as Gracie. I'd never seen her look scared before, not ever. She was even cool when the staff guys were taking down Jackson. But now she was shaking from fear.

"Don't cut me," she begged.

"I don't *want* to, but if you don't come nice and easy, then I've *got* to. You get the program?"

"Yeah, yeah," Jenna said.

The two of them got up, both looking up.

"Just keep smiling at the camera," Sig told her. "Gracie, I want your pass-card. Just hand it over so the camera can't see."

This was like some weird movie. Sig got the pass-card from Gracie, and maybe that could get him outside. But what then? What kind of plan did Sig have?

Sig and Jenna began moving across the room, smiling like crazy. The rest of us were frozen in our

60

desks. When they got halfway to the door, Jenna
began shaking from sheer terror.

"Stop it," Sig ordered. "Stop it or I'll have to –"

I didn't let Sig finish his threat. "Sig, let her go,"
I told him. I tried to keep my voice calm and easy.
"You need a hostage, but you don't need her. She's
falling apart already. Let her go and take me."

This came like a brainwave. It even surprised
me.

I could see Sig trying to figure out what to do.
He could drag a crying girl with him, or he could

have me. The choice seemed pretty simple. The only problem was that I might get killed along the way.

"Okay, come here," Sig told me.

I got up and walked to Sig and Jenna. We were all trying to act like this was normal, like we were a bunch of actors doing a scene from a play. Except this play was real life. The knife in Sig's hand was a real knife. And the fear in my gut was real fear, for a real good reason.

"Okay, let her go," I whispered.

He did. Jenna ran back to her desk just as Sig brought the knife across my chest. It was the first time I ever felt a blade up against my neck.

Sig looked up. "Now, Gracie, I'm sorry about this, but I've got a job for you. Here, take these matches," he said, throwing a pack to her. "I want you to start a little fire in the waste basket, you got it?"

"Sig, this is crazy. It's not going to work," Gracie told him.

"Maybe not, but I'm going to give it my best shot," he said. His voice was calm. "Now you start a fire. Strike a match or else I'm going to see whether Russ here bleeds a little or bleeds a lot."

Gracie didn't have any choice. Her hands were shaking as she struck the match. When it caught, she threw the match into the waste basket. Nothing happened. She struck another match, then held this one against a sheet of paper. At last the paper caught fire. In a few minutes, the whole waste basket was smoking like crazy.

"Okay, Russ, you pull the fire alarm," Sig told me. "We're getting out of here."

CHAPTER 8

Break Out

I had to give Sig some credit – his plan wasn't bad. The fire alarm would open up all the locked doors. There was no way they could lock us inside Juvie if the place was on fire. If that didn't work, Gracie's pass-card would open the door. Sig's plan wouldn't get us outside the fence, but it would get us down the hall.

To get outside the fence, he'd have to use me.

Sig grabbed me around the neck and dragged

me sideways down the hall. It was like I was a big suitcase that he was dragging with him. He had one arm around my neck, the other arm and hand holding the knife. Behind us, we left the class and a bunch of smoke coming up from a waste can.

The classrooms were in the Hub. To get from the Hub to outside, we had to go through a long tunnel made of wire mesh. There were metal doors on both sides of the tunnel. We made it out from the classroom, out from the Hub and into the tunnel. So far, Sig's plan was working.

"Hey, let go," I told him after a while. His arm came up and choked me every so often, and I didn't like it. "We'll go faster if I can walk. I promise I won't take off on you."

"You're the hostage," he said.

"Yeah, but I'm a better hostage if I can breathe. If you really need a shield or something, grab me. Otherwise, let's just go."

This must have made sense. He let go of my neck and the two of us ran down the tunnel. For a second, I thought this might get me into trouble. I mean, a hostage doesn't have any choice. But a guy

who's just going along with the escape, well, they might nail me, too.

Still, there wasn't a lot of time to think. I'd rather run than choke. Besides, Sig didn't need me as a hostage right then. He needed to move.

We ran down the tunnel fast. There was a fire alarm making its *clang-clang-clang* as we ran. At the far end, I saw the door to the entry hall. Beyond that was one more door, the one that led outside. Two doors and Sig would be free. Two doors and Sig would be out in the real world. The first door was still locked, but Gracie's pass-card got it open. The last door was locked, but it stayed locked. The guys in the control room had got the plan figured out.

That's when Sig grabbed me again. "Open it or I'll cut him," he shouted at a camera.

The blade felt cold against my neck. It was sharp, too. I could feel it slice in, just a little.

"Open it!" Sig yelled again.

But nothing happened. The door stayed locked.

"Hey, it doesn't pay to cut me," I told him. "These guys in the control room don't care. You'll just end up in the pen."

Sig swore.

"Okay, Plan B," he told me.

He stopped cold, and so did I. We ran back into the tunnel. When we got halfway, Sig stopped. In front of us there was a metal grate that led to the yard. I'd never seen the grate open. I had a hunch that it was shut for all time. But my hunch was wrong.

Sig went to one side of the tunnel, then ran against the door. SMASH! The door burst open.

"How'd you do that?" I asked him.

"I cut the lock last week when I was on yard duty," he said. "Just in case."

I was impressed. Not only did Sig have a Plan B, but Plan B might just work. Guys like Jackson are so stupid they only have one plan. They pay off a staff guy and think that's good enough. They make a break for it, something goes wrong, and they're toast. But Sig had some real brain power. His Plan A was pretty good. Now his Plan B got us to the yard. The trouble was, we were still inside the fence.

It was cold, wet and foggy when we popped out of the tunnel. We could still hear the fire alarm, but now there was a new sound – the escape siren.

"What now?" I asked him.

"To the fence, man," he shot back.

The fence around Juvie wasn't like the wall around a pen, or anything like that. It was just your basic chain-link fence with the top bent over like a candy cane. But that candy-cane top just made it impossible to climb.

We made it to the fence pretty quick. In the

fog, it came up on us so fast we ran right into it. Then we stopped. I thought Sig was going to start climbing, but he didn't. Instead, Sig ran along the fence until he found a storm sewer. It was half filled from the rain, but you could still squeeze through it.

"Not bad," I told him, looking at the sewer. "I like your Plan B."

"There's a car out there, waiting. So are you coming with me?"

"I can't do it, Sig," I told him. "I'm too gutless." That was only half true. Maybe if I had a long sentence like Sig or Jackson, maybe I'd run for it. Maybe if being locked up was just too much for me, maybe I'd run. But I only had ten months to go, maybe less. Why risk all that – and risk my life too?

"Last chance, Russ. I got a buddy out there."

"No thanks, man," I told him.

"Your call," he said, still waiting.

He might have said a little more, but we both heard voices and running steps coming closer. The fog was so thick we couldn't see anything, but we heard them coming.

"Give it up, kid," shouted one of the staff guys.

Sig grabbed me, as quick as anything. He had his arm around my neck and his knife aimed at my throat.

"Don't come closer," Sig shouted. "You come closer and Russ starts to bleed." He was shouting into the fog. He couldn't see the staff guys. And I wondered if they could see us.

"Let him go," came another shout. I knew the voice. It was Stick Man.

"No way," Sig shouted back. "You start anything and you'll have a dead body out here. Try to explain that one, Stick Man. We all know that you suckered Jackson and the D-wing guys. You think you can get away with that twice?"

It was quiet. There was no sound but the siren and our heavy breathing.

Sig whispered in my ear, "Better start talking to them." Then he let me go and slid into the storm sewer.

"He's got a knife at my throat," I told them. This wasn't exactly true, but I figured they couldn't see us that well. "He says he'll kill me if you come any closer. Why don't you just let him go? He didn't hurt anybody back there."

There were some whispers out in the fog. Then I heard another voice, not Stick Man's. "We're going to give you ten seconds to let him go, Sig. You hear us? Ten seconds."

I didn't like this. What were they going to do in ten seconds? The staff always told us they didn't have guns. But was that the truth?

"Nine . . . eight . . . seven."

By now, Sig must be down at the road, getting into his buddy's car. Or else he was running like crazy to the highway. But what about these staff guys? Did they have guns aimed at me? What kind of plan did the staff have?

"Six . . . five . . . four . . . let him go, Sig."

"It's okay!" I yelled out. "He put the knife down!"

The voice seemed to be smiling. "Then walk toward us, both of you. No funny stuff."

So I walked slowly toward the voice. Step, step, step. Might as well give Sig as much time as I could.

In no time, I could see the staff guys and they

could see me. There were no guns. Just a bunch of guys with cuffs and the blanket.

"Where'd he go?" asked the voice.

"Beats me," I told them. "He was right behind me a second ago."

CHAPTER 9

Two Kinds of Freedom

The staff had a million questions. I think they grilled me for the rest of that day and most of the next. I kept telling them the truth, mostly. Sure, Sig told us all that he wanted to break out. Sure, Sig told me he was making a break that day. No, I didn't believe him. No one ever believed Sig.

Yes, he had a knife on me. Yes, I took Jenna's place as a hostage. No, that was not part of some big plan. No, I never wanted to be part of the escape. No, I didn't help Sig get away.

I tried to answer all their questions as best I could. I knew the staff was angry. They had been out-smarted by one of the inmates, one of the kids. It wasn't supposed to happen like that. Then there was the stuff Sig had said about Stick Man. It was true, of course. But I bet he didn't like hearing it out loud.

At last, they had to let me go. What were they going to do? Throw me into Juvie? Besides, I had risked my life to save one of the other kids. In a lot of places, I would have gotten a medal.

I did get a round of applause when I got back to C wing. Kareem came up a slapped me on the shoulders. "My man!" he said, which was pretty high praise coming from him.

Mouse, of course, had lots to say. "You were a hero. I mean, you risked your life for that chick, what's her name?"

"Jenna."

"Yeah, right," he went on. "I tell you, when you

both get out of here, she's going to be real grateful. You're going to do okay, Russ."

"Yeah, when I get out," I sighed.

There was no word on Sig. His Plan B had been a good one, and his break looked pretty clean. Somebody was waiting for him outside the fence. Somebody got him into a car and took him right out of town. He had made it, we thought. Crazy Sig had made it outside.

Then we found out what really happened.

We were all sitting in front of the TV, watching *Newsworld*. That was one of the shows staff would let us watch. The "breaking news" that night was a car crash, a big one.

"One youth is dead and one is clinging to life tonight," it began. There was a picture of a burning car. All around it were RCMP.

"A fiery crash cost one young man his life today," it went on. "Another has first-degree burns. Some reports say that the car was being pursued by the police when it left the road."

My jaw dropped. I think all of us in C wing stopped breathing.

"The car burst into flames after leaving the road. Police were on the scene but unable to rescue the driver."

"Some reports say that the car was part of a jail-break at the Broken Arrow Correction Centre two days ago. The name of the dead youth has not yet been released by police. He may have been an inmate at the Correction Centre. Tune in for more details at eleven."

Nobody said a thing. Nobody could make a

joke, or shed a tear. We were stunned. The news hit us that hard.

Back in the room, after lights out, Mouse said just one thing. "Sig wanted to get out of here," he said, trying hard not to break down. "He wanted to be free."

"The guy got his wish," I said. Then it was my turn to fight back a sob.

CHAPTER 10

Sprung

A month later, I got a call from my lawyer. He was a young guy, just out of law school. The trouble was, he wasn't much of a lawyer. He's just one of those guys the court gives you for free. He was coming by with some news. I shrugged. Maybe he was going to appeal my sentence. Maybe he was going to get me into a group home faster. Who knew?

So on the next visiting day, I met with him in

this "talk" room we have. He was on one side of the glass, I was on the other.

"You're going home, Russ," he told me with a big smile on his face.

"Yeah, right," I said. I'd been kind of down since Sig died. Now I didn't trust anybody or anything.

"I'm not kidding," the lawyer told me. "The cops picked up some guy called Flick. They were grilling him on something else, and then he told them all about the accident."

"You mean the accident that got blamed on me?"

"Yeah. Turns out that Flick was behind the wheel, not you."

Big surprise, I thought to myself. I could have told him that months ago, but I wasn't going to rat.

"Anyhow, the judge threw out your sentence."

"So I'm clear?" I asked.

"Not exactly. You were still part of the crime. An accessory."

I knew the word. It's a big word for somebody who was part of a crime but not the leader and not the brains. An accessory just goes along for the ride. But an accessory gets a warning, not time in Juvie.

The lawyer went on. "So you still have a record, at least until you're 18. But the good news is that you're out of here, Russ. Get your stuff together. Your parents are going to pick you up in two hours, just as soon as I file some papers."

So what do you do when somebody tells you this? Do you laugh, or shout, or scream? I just sat there, my mouth open, looking stunned. I didn't believe it – and I did believe it – both at once.

The truth will out! Shakespeare said that in a play we did with Gracie. I had started to wonder about that. I'd been in Juvie for three months, and the truth stayed pretty well hidden. But now Flick had told the cops, or had been forced to tell the cops, and I was going to be free. I was going home.

I got back to C wing while the others were still in class. It was really quiet on the wing, and there was nobody to talk to. Old Pops, the staff guy, was home that day. We hadn't seen Stick Man since the day Sig got out. Gracie was off teaching in the Hub, off with Jenna and Kareem.

But I wanted to say goodbye to somebody. I couldn't just go off like I didn't care. These guys in C wing, and Jenna too, had started to mean something to me. It's not like we were buddies, but we had been through a lot. I'd never forget them. I didn't want them to forget me. But there was no way I could see all of them before I left. So I picked the most important one.

I knocked on the classroom door before going in. It was the "blue" group, with some teacher I didn't know. Behind the glass door I could see Mouse with a pencil and some kind of workbook. After a little talk with the teacher, Mouse came to the door.

"Hey, what's up, Russ?" he asked outside.

Up over our heads, cameras were watching us. Down the hall, staff guys were listening.

"I got sprung," I told him. "Flick told the cops what happened. So now I'm a free man. I'm going home."

There was a smile on Mouse's face, but his eyes looked like he was going to cry.

"No kidding?" he asked.

"No kidding."

We both stood there, kind of awkward, kind of happy, kind of sad.

"I'm gonna miss you," he said. "Who's gonna read to me?"

"You've got to read for yourself, man. I left *Holes* on your bed. I mean, I read it to you three times so you must know the thing by heart now. You can do it, Mouse. It's not that hard."

"Yeah, but I'm still gonna miss you, Russ. Things are changing around here. Sig is gone and you're leaving. There's just gonna be me and Kareem . . ."

"And Jenna," I reminded him. "I think she's got

the hots for you, Mouse. She might seem kind of cold, but I think she has her eye on you."

Mouse just laughed and I shook his hand. I wanted all this to end with a laugh, because we hadn't had enough of those. You don't get to laugh much in Juvie. That's one more reason I never want to go back.

EPILOGUE

All that was five years ago. I got out of Juvie and kept my nose clean and picked my friends better. Maybe that's how I was able to finish high school. I tried a couple of stupid jobs, like selling cell phones at the mall. But then I heard they needed staff at Juvie. So now I'm back, on the other side of the locked doors. Pretty funny, eh?

My buddy Mouse really did learn to read. He read some real easy books, then finished *Holes* on his own. He never finished high school but got an okay job at a supermarket in town. He doesn't go to visit his dad any more. Maybe that's why he hangs out with me.

Kareem got out of Juvie and went to a group home. Then he went back to his family. Last I heard, he got a job as a welder out in B.C.

I heard that Jenna finished her time in Juvie, but then hit the streets. She got hooked on crack and now spends her time in and out of rehab. It's too bad, if you ask me. That girl was something, and could have been something special.

Stick Man got caught stealing money from inmates. He got fired from Juvie and then we lost track of him. I wouldn't be surprised to see him behind bars some day.

And then there was Gracie. Our best teacher was really shaken up by Sig's breakout. I bet she'd never had to face a guy with a knife before. Anyhow, she stopped teaching at Juvie and now teaches in a regular school. I ran into her at the mall one day, and she says she misses some of the old guys, like Mouse and me.

"Glad to see you doing so well," she told me.

"You, too, Gracie. How do you like the kids you teach now? What's it like teaching Grade 7?"

Gracie shook her head. "Some days," she sighed, "I think I'd rather be back at Juvie."

Playing Chicken by PAUL KROPP

Josh just wanted to fit in with the guys. It should have been a whole summer of wild nights, but then Guzzo dares him to a race that ends everything.

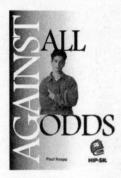

Against All Odds
by PAUL KROPP

Nothing ever came easy for Jeff. He had a tough time at school and hung around with all the wrong kids in the neighborhood. But when he and his brother are drowning in a storm sewer, Jeff is the one who never gives up.

Avalanche
by PAUL KROPP

It was just a school trip, just a winter hike through the mountains. But when a wall of snow comes sliding down, fifteen kids have to fight for their lives. Not all of them will win the fight.

Show Off by PAUL KROPP

Nikki was one tough girl, or so all the kids said. She'd take on anybody, risk anything for the gang. But that was before she met Austin and began to turn her life around.

Ghost House by PAUL KROPP

Tyler and Zach don't believe in ghosts. So when a friend offers them big money to spend a night in the old Blackwood house, they jump at the chance. There's no such thing as ghosts, right?

Terror 9/11 by DOUG PATON

Seventeen-year-old Jason was just picking up his sister at the World Trade Centre when the first plane hit. As the towers burst into flames, he has to struggle to save his sister, his dad and himself.

Street Scene by PAUL KROPP

The guys weren't looking for trouble. Maybe Dwayne did pick the wrong girl to dance with. But did that give Sal and his gang an excuse to come after them? The fight should never have started – and it should never have finished the way it did.

Hitting the Road
by PAUL KROPP

The road isn't nice to kids who run away. Matt knew there would be trouble even before he took off with his friend Cody. Along the way, there would be fighting, fear, hunger and a jump from a speeding train. Was it all worth it?

Student Narc
by PAUL KROPP

It wasn't Kevin's idea to start working with the cops. But when his best friend dies from an overdose, somebody has to do something. Kevin finally takes on a whole drug gang – and their boss – in a struggle that leaves him scarred for life.

About the Author

Paul Kropp is the author of many popular novels for young people. His work includes six award-winning young-adult novels, many high-interest novels, as well as writing for adults and younger children.

Mr. Kropp's best-known novels for young adults, *Moonkid and Prometheus* and *Moonkid and Liberty*, have been translated into German, Danish, French, Portuguese and two dialects of Spanish. They have won awards both in Canada and abroad. His most recent books are *Running the Bases* (Doubleday) *The Countess and Me* (Fitzhenry and Whiteside), both young-adult novels, and *What a Story!* (Scholastic), a picture book for young children.

Paul Kropp lives with his wife, Lori, in an 1889 town-house in Toronto's Cabbagetown district.

For more information, see the author's website at
www.paulkropp.com

For more information on HIP books, contact:

 High Interest Publishing – Publishers of H·I·P Books
www.hip-books.com